For Tommy, Billy, Emma and Katie – J.D.

First published 2000 by Macmillan Children's Books
This edition published 2016 by Macmillan Children's Books
an imprint of Pan Macmillan
The Smithson, 6 Briset Street, London EC1M 5NR
Associated companies throughout the world
www.panmacmillan.com

ISBN 978-1-5098-1249-3

15 14

A CIP catalogue record for this book is available
from the British Library.

Printed in China

FSC
www.fsc.org

MIX
Paper from
responsible sources
FSC® C116313

WRITTEN BY
JULIA DONALDSON

ILLUSTRATED BY
AXEL SCHEFFLER

Monkey Puzzle

MACMILLAN CHILDREN'S BOOKS

"I've lost my mum!"

"Hush, little monkey, don't you cry.
I'll help you find her," said Butterfly.
"Let's have a think. How big is she?"

"She's big!" said the monkey. "Bigger than me."

"Bigger than you? Then I've seen your mum.
Come, little monkey, come, come, come."

"No, no, no! That's an elephant.

"My mum isn't a great grey hunk.
She hasn't got tusks or a curly trunk.
She doesn't have great thick baggy knees.
And anyway, *her* tail coils round trees."

"She coils round trees? Then she's very near.
Quick, little monkey! She's over here."

"No, no, no! That's a snake.

"Mum doesn't look a *bit* like this.
She doesn't slither about and hiss.
She doesn't curl round a nest of eggs.
And anyway, my mum's got more legs."

"It's legs *we're* looking for now, you say?
I know where she is, then. Come this way."

"No, no, no! That's a spider.

"Mum isn't black and hairy and fat.
She's not got so many legs as *that!*
She'd rather eat fruit than swallow a fly,
And she lives in the treetops, way up high."

"She lives in the trees? You should have said!
Your mummy's hiding above your head."

"No, no, no! That's a parrot.

"Mum's got a nose and not a beak.
She doesn't squawk and squabble and shriek.
She doesn't have claws or feathery wings.
And anyway, my mum leaps and springs."

"Aha! I've got it! She leaps about?

She's just round the corner, without a doubt."

"No, no, no! That's a frog!

"Butterfly, butterfly, please don't joke!
Mum's not green and she doesn't croak.
She's not all slimy. Oh dear, what a muddle!
She's brown and furry, and nice to cuddle."

"Brown fur – why didn't you tell me so?
We'll find her in no time – off we go!"

"No, no, no! That's a bat.

"Why do you keep on getting it wrong?
Mum doesn't sleep the whole day long.
I told you, she's got no wings at all,
And anyway, she's not *nearly* so small!"

"Your mum's not little? Now let me think.
She's down by the river, having a drink!"

"NO, NO, NO!
That's the elephant again!

"Butterfly, butterfly, can't you see?
None of these creatures looks like me!"

"You never told me she looked like you!"

"Of course I didn't! I thought you knew!"

"I didn't know. I couldn't! You see . . .

". . . None of my babies looks like me.

So she looks like you! Well, if that's *the case*

We'll soon discover her hiding place."

"No, no, no! That's my dad!"

"Come, little monkey, come, come, come.

It's time I took you home to . . ."

"Mum!"